This igloo book belongs to:

igloobooks

Published in 2017
by Igloo Books Ltd
Cottage Farm
Sywell
NN6 0BJ
www.igloobooks.com

REX001 0517
2 4 6 8 10 9 7 5 3
ISBN: 978-1-78343-826-6

Written by Jo Lacey
Illustrated by Gail Yerrill

Cover designed by Lee Italiano
Interiors designed by Stephanie Drake
Edited by Stephanie Moss

Printed and manufactured in China

A New Friend for Mouse

igloobooks

Here is Mouse. This is her new house.
It's nestled in the root of an old oak tree.

WELCOME

Come and see...

... She's got a mousey bed at the top of the stairs and a mousey table and mousey chairs. Mouse should be happy, but she feels sad.

Mouse, why do you **feel** so bad?

Mouse says, "No one comes to visit me at all.
I think it's because I'm so very small."

Drip,

drop.

Oh, dear. Is that a tear?

Suddenly, THUMP,

THUMP,

THUMP!

Who is that, stomping past?

"A visitor!" cries Mouse.

"At last!"

She dashes out, squeaking,

"Hello, I'm down here!"

There is an elephant, quaking with fear.

"Urgh! A mouse!" cries Elephant.
"Don't come near me."

Mouse takes tiny steps,
one, two, three.

There's a terrified TRUMPET!

Elephant runs away.
"Come back!" cries Mouse.
"I only want to play."

"Don't hide," says Mouse. "Please talk to me.
I'm really very kind. Come down. You'll see."

"You'll tickle my trunk," replies Elephant.
"You'll run to the top.

You'll scurry around
and the tickling won't stop."

Mouse sits very quietly.

She thinks for a while.

What are you thinking, Mouse?

Why that smile?

"I'll make you a treat,"
she says to Elephant.

"Come with me. I won't run up your trunk.

I promise. You'll see."

"Er... okay," says Elephant.
He follows, feeling suspicious.

Then, he tastes Mouse's cupcakes
and they are delicious.

She makes strawberry muffins
and warm, acorn pie.

"Yummy,"
says Elephant, with
a contented sigh.

Elephant says, "Let's have some **fun.**"

They skip and slide.

They jump and run.

They play catch the tail,

hide-and-seek and chase.

They run around, giggling, all over the place.

"Climb up my trunk," says Elephant.
"We're going for a ride."
He sways his great trunk
from side to side.

Elephant walks **proudly** along the track.
"**Look!**" he cries...

... "I've got a mouse on my back."

"WOW!" cries Mouse,
at the animals below.
She wiggles her whisker
and squeaks, "Hello!"

Mouse is so happy because she isn't alone.
"Come on," says Elephant.
"It's time to go home."

"Thank you," whispers Mouse,
giving Elephant's ear a tug.
"If I wasn't so small,
I'd give you a hug."

Oh, Mouse, you must be happy,
now you have a new friend.

"Yes, very happy," replies Mouse, "goodbye."

THE END.